View from the Top

by
Paul McCusker

Augustine Institute

Greenwood Village, CO

Augustine Institute
6160 S. Syracuse Way, Suite 310
Greenwood Village, CO 80111
Tel: (866) 767-3155
www.augustineinstitute.org

Note: Different versions of some of these stories
have appeared in the *Signs of Grace* series.

Print Production: Joseph Pearce,
Grace Hagan, Amy Schell
Creative Director: Ben Dybas
Cover Design: Lisa Marie Patterson
Illustrations: Robert Dunn

ISBN 978-1-7338598-5-1
Library of Congress Control Number 2019941514

Printed in Canada ∞

Contents

Introduction   5

1. Flaps   9

2. Rejoice   25

3. Car Talk   39

4. Paper Balls   47

5. Being Happy   61

6. Exitus   75

7. Discovery   83

8. Seeing Things   97

9. Near and Far   105

10. In Focus, Out of Control   117

11. Seeing Clearly   129

12. A New View   139

13. Be Ye Glad   155

14. The Big Game   171

15. Again I Say Rejoice   183

Introduction

Nicholas and Samantha Perry are twins. Nicholas is usually called Nick and Samantha is called Sam. They are both eight years old. They live in Hope Springs in Colorado. It is a town that has a lot of fun things to do.

Nick and Sam attend the St. Clare of Assisi Catholic Church and its school. Their teacher is Sister Lucy. The twins like Sister Lucy a lot.

Father Cliff Montgomery is the pastor at St. Clare's. He is young and full of energy. Deacon Chuck Crosby is older and helps Father Cliff a lot. Norm Sullivan is the handyman for the church and the school. He is friendly and has an unusual way of thinking about things.

Nick's best friends are Brad and Riley. Brad sometimes leads Nick and Sam into trouble. Riley is interested in things like Big Foot, aliens, conspiracies, and other far-out things.

Sam's best friend is Kim. Kim was born in China. She now lives in Hope Springs with her aunt and uncle.

Nick and Sam have a ten-year-old sister named Lizzy. Lizzy is short for Elizabeth. They also have a twelve-year-old brother named Andrew. Their parents are named Jon and Belle.

Nick and Sam like Hope Springs. Their father's family has lived there for over a hundred years. They're glad they left the big city of Denver to settle there.

Our stories tell about Nick's and Sam's life, adventures, and struggles in Hope Springs. Maybe their lives are a lot like yours.

CHAPTER ONE

—•—

Flaps

Nick Perry and his best friend Brad were playing catch on the front lawn of the Perry's house.

It was not going well for Nick. Catching the ball was no problem. Throwing the ball back was hard. The ball often went too far to the left or too far to the right or too high or too low. Brad would chase it.

"I'm getting tired of this game," Brad called out after he'd picked up the ball yet again.

Nick once hoped he would become a great baseball player. But playing catch with Brad made him think he should consider doing something else.

Brad threw the ball back to Nick. Then he held up his glove and said, "Now, *aim carefully* and throw it to my glove."

Nick held the ball tightly in his right hand. He looked at Brad's glove and then Brad's face and then Brad's glove. He drew back his arm and with all his strength threw the ball.

The ball shot to the left and over Brad's head. Brad reached up as high as he could. The ball sailed past.

The ball hit the ground and bounced past the front porch just as Sam, Nick's twin sister, stepped out. She saw the ball roll toward the neighbor's yard.

Brad frowned at Nick.

"The sun was in my eyes," Nick said.

Brad looked up at the cloudy sky. He

looked at Nick. "I'm not playing catch anymore."

"I'll get it," Sam said. She jumped down the porch steps and ran to the neighbor's yard. She picked up the ball.

Brad held up his glove. "Here," he said.

Sam threw the ball. It went over Brad's head.

"You're as bad as your brother," he complained.

The ball flew straight to Nick. He caught it in his glove.

"I wasn't throwing it to you," Sam said to Brad as she walked back to the porch.

Brad looked surprised. "That was a good throw," he said.

"Thanks," she said.

Brad ran over to Nick and took the ball. "Do that again," he said. He tossed the ball underhand to Sam. She caught it in her cupped hands.

"Do what again?" Sam asked.

Brad moved to the far edge of the lawn. He waved for Nick to spread out toward the sidewalk. "Throw it to me," Brad said. He held up his glove.

Sam looked at the ball, then looked up at Brad. She threw the ball again. It flew straight to Brad. He hardly had to move his glove to catch it.

"You're really good," Brad said. He looked over at Nick.

"You mean she's better than me," Nick said.

Brad walked the ball back to Sam. "Let's do it again," he said.

"I didn't come out to play catch." Sam turned to Nick. "Nick, Dad wants me to tell you—"

Before she could finish her sentence, the loud roar of a truck engine echoed down the street. The two boys spun around to look.

A large truck came into view. The

front cab was a bright red. It pulled a long trailer that was white with black trim. On the side, in red letters that matched the front cab, were the words "Kraft's Moving Company."

Nick gasped and turned to Sam. "We're moving *today*? But we can't move so fast! We just decided!"

Sam laughed. "They're dropping off boxes," she said.

Brad turned to Nick. "You're *moving*?"

"We're not moving today," Sam said again.

The moving truck pulled along the curb.

"You're moving?" Brad looked angry.

Just then the garage door lifted up. Jon Perry, the twins' father, stepped out. He waved at the driver of the truck and walked over to talk to him.

"You're moving," Brad said to Nick.

"I thought I told you," Nick said.

Brad glared at Nick. "You're moving!"

I guess I didn't, Nick thought.

***

Nick and Brad stood in the garage. The family's two cars had been moved to the street. A couple of stacks of collapsed moving boxes took up the center of the cement floor. Nick's dad had said that packing up most of their belongings themselves would save a lot of money. The boxes had to be assembled. That would be the twins' job.

"Why are you moving?" Brad asked.

"We're renting this house," Nick explained. "We planned to live here until we found a real house."

"Where did you find a real house?" Brad asked.

"It's the Old Perry House," Nick replied.

Brad gasped. "You're moving into *that* thing?"

"What's wrong with it?"

"It's *ancient!*" Brad said. "It has to

be, like, a *hundred* years old."

Nick remembered his dad saying that the house was built in a style that had something to do with a queen in England. "It was built by Queen Victoria," Nick said. "Or someone like that."

"Why are you moving into that old thing?" Brad asked.

"My Uncle Clark has been living there all by himself. It's too big for him. He wants to live up in the mountains, close to the resort he's building."

"So?"

"So, my parents don't want him to sell the house. My dad grew up in it. The same with his father. And *his* father." Nick had lost count of how many "greats" to put in front of the "grandfathers" who were part of the Perry history. "So we're moving in."

"Is your family rich?" Brad asked. "I mean, your uncle is building that hotel and golf course and ski slopes and all of those cabins on the mountain."

The Pine Creek Pass Resort caused a lot of arguments in Hope Springs. Uncle Clark said it will bring tourists and jobs to the town. Some people like Brad's father said it would ruin the natural beauty of the mountain.

Brad eyed him. "Are *you* rich?" he asked.

Nick thought about the 37 cents he had in his pocket. "No," he said.

Brad kicked at the edge of a box. "When are you going to move?" he asked.

"After school ends," Nick replied. That was only a month from now. There was a lot to do.

The door leading into the house opened. Belle Perry, Nick's mother, came out. She was carrying something in her hand that had a large green handle with a big round wheel on top.

Sam was following her. She was carrying another green-handled thing.

"It's time to start putting the boxes together," Mrs. Perry said.

The boys moved out of the way.

"Pick up one of the boxes," Mrs. Perry said as she grabbed a collapsed box. "Turn it on its edge so the writing is upside down. Push the sides outward."

The cardboard took the shape of a square box with flaps on both ends.

She folded down the two flaps on the top and pushed them together. "This is the bottom of the box," she said. Then she held up the thing with the large green handle.

Nick now saw that the big wheel on top was a roll of clear tape.

"This is the packing tape dispenser," Mrs. Perry said. She pressed the wheel against the side of the box. It made a loud *ripping* sound as she pulled the tape across the bottom flaps to seal them together.

The dispenser had a line of metal teeth that tore the tape from the roll, just like the small tape dispenser in Nick's room.

Mrs. Perry flipped the box right-side up. "Tah dah!" she said. "That's all there is to it."

Nick looked at the stacks of boxes. "There must be a hundred boxes here," he said. He looked at Brad.

Brad gave a panicked smile. "I have to go home," he suddenly said. He rushed out, grabbing his baseball glove as he went.

"Coward!" Nick shouted after him.

"It's just the two of you. We have a lot of packing to do and can't start until we have boxes," Mrs. Perry said. She left Nick and Sam to start the assembly line.

Nick picked up the green-handled tape dispenser. "This is cool," he said. "It's like a space-age blaster."

"Don't mess around," Sam said.

Nick imagined aliens were crawling out from behind the junk in the garage.

"Come on," Sam said. She seemed to have a knack for box-making. Flip over, push out, flaps down, tape the bottom, right-side up, and the box was made. "Tape the bottom of this."

Nick pressed the sticky part of the tape against the side of the box. He pulled up. The tape came off. He tried again, pressing harder. He pulled up and over to tape the bottom flaps together. The dispenser veered to the left.

"A *straight* line," Sam said.

"I'm trying!" Nick said. He tried to

put the tape straight again. There was a terrible grinding noise. "Aliens," he said.

"Hurry up," Sam said impatiently.

Nick pulled the tape to the other end of the flaps and down the side. The metal teeth didn't cut the tape off. Nick pulled. More tape ripped from the roll. "It won't let go," Nick said.

"Give me that," Sam said and took the green handle from him. She tore the tape across the teeth and stuck what was left onto the box. "*There*," she said.

Nick felt annoyed. "You should do them all since you're so good at it," he said.

"Don't pout," she said. She pushed the tape dispenser into his hands. "It's not that hard. I'll show you."

"I'll do something else," he said.

"But Mom said to do this," Sam said. "You'll get in trouble if you don't help."

Nick looked at the large long rolls of gray paper nearby. "I'll take the rolls of packing paper to our rooms. Mom said we need them to wrap everything up before they go into the boxes."

Sam looked unhappy. "It's up to you."

Nick picked up a roll of packing paper. It was heavier than he thought. The front end tipped to the floor. He tucked it tighter under his arm. The back end toppled to the floor.

Sam put a hand over her mouth to stop a giggle.

Nick snorted at her and cradled the roll in both arms like a baby. That seemed to work. He carried the roll into the house. He had to be careful not to catch the ends on the door jam.

He continued into the kitchen.

His older brother Andrew was standing in front of the refrigerator. "What happened to all the juice?" he asked.

"Beats me," Nick said with a strained voice.

Andrew looked over at him and

laughed. "That looks like a propeller on an airplane," he said.

"It's heavy," Nick said. He went to the hall and started up the stairs. The roll wobbled. His arms hurt.

"Do you need help?" Andrew called from the kitchen.

"I'm not helpless!" Nick shouted back. But halfway up the stairs, the front end of the roll of paper hit the bannister. It wrenched from Nick's arms and fell. There was a *bang* as it hit the stairs and then slid down to the main floor.

Andrew rounded the corner. "Let me help," he said.

"*No!*" Nick shouted. He grabbed the end of the paper roll and crab-walked it up the stairs. It bumped loudly against each step.

Andrew watched him with his arms folded and a smirk on his face.

Nick got the roll to the top and

dropped it in the upstairs hallway. He sat down on the floor.

Andrew laughed and went back to the kitchen.

Nick saw a piece of tape flapping from his elbow. In a rage he grabbed it and tried to toss it aside. It stuck to his fingers. He shook his hand hard. The tape wouldn't let go. He tried to roll it into a ball. Part of the tape stuck to his fingers and another part stuck to his leg.

"You can move without me!" Nick shouted to anyone who might be listening. "I'm staying right here!"

CHAPTER TWO

—.—

Rejoice

The next day at St. Clare's Catholic School, Sam sat next to her friend Kim in the morning assembly. Kim looked sad.

"What's wrong?" Sam asked her.

Kim pulled a folded piece of paper from her sweater pocket. She unfolded it. "I got a letter from my father," she said.

Sam saw Chinese writing on the page.

Kim was born in China but lived with her aunt and uncle in Hope Springs. Her parents were still in China. They were Catholics who had been put in jail for their faith. The Chinese leaders did that to try to stop people from believing in Jesus and his Church.

"My mother has been sick," Kim said.

Sam felt bad for her friend and gave her a hug. "Is it bad?"

Kim shrugged. "The letter didn't say what was wrong. I'm worried."

Sam nodded. *Who wouldn't be?*

"But I shouldn't be worried," Kim said. "I should be happy."

Sam was puzzled. "Happy? Why should you be happy that your mother is sick?"

Kim pointed to a line of writing on the paper. "My father put a Bible verse at the end of the letter. My aunt and uncle said it's from a letter St. Paul wrote to a church in a place called . . . " Kim spoke slowly, "*Phil-ip-pie.* It's in chapter four, verse four."

"What does it say?" Sam asked.

"St. Paul said, 'Rejoice in the Lord

always, again I say rejoice.'" She folded the paper up again and put it in her pocket. She asked, "How am I supposed to rejoice all the time?"

Sam heard the word "rejoice" a lot in church and in Bible lessons. She thought it meant to be happy, but she wasn't sure. *Can a person be happy all of the time?*

"My mom is sick while she's in jail with my dad. How am I supposed to rejoice always?" Kim asked. "But I have to, because my dad said so."

Father Cliff Montgomery stepped up to the microphone. "In the name of the Father, and the Son, and the Holy Spirit," he said as he did the Sign of the Cross. The room went silent and the kids followed him.

Father Cliff led them in morning prayer. Then he stepped aside for Sister Stephanie, the school principal, to give announcements.

"Good morning," Sister Stephanie said with a bright smile. "It's almost time for our big end-of-the-school-year event . . . the *spring festival!*"

Some of the students cheered. This was Sam's first year at St. Clare's. She didn't know what a spring festival was.

Sister Stephanie held up a colorful poster. "This year's festival is called 'Be Ye Glad.' I think it's going to be the best one ever. We're going to have contests and games and costumes and fun rides. Your teachers will tell you more in your classes. I hope you'll all volunteer to help."

Sam looked at Kim. Kim's head was lowered, and she clutched the letter in her hands. Sam wondered, *How is anyone supposed to rejoice always?*

***

Sister Lucy hung up a spring festival poster next to the board in the front of the third-grade class. Sam could see the words "Be Ye Glad" in the middle of a painting of brightly colored flowers, the smiling faces of children, a picnic spread, and a lot of smaller images that looked like families having fun.

It's easy to rejoice when you're doing things like that, Sam thought. She glanced at Kim.

Kim looked at her and forced a small smile.

Sister Lucy pointed to the poster. "Be Ye Glad is going to have a Robin Hood theme," she said. "We're going to dress up like people did in those days."

"Will we get to shoot arrows?" Riley asked.

That's just the kind of thing Riley would think about, Sam thought. Riley sat next to her in class and was one of Nick's best friends.

Sister Lucy smiled. "There will be an archery contest with the kind of arrows that have Velcro tips. We'll have sword fights—with the *sponge*-type swords," she added quickly, to stop Riley's next question.

Riley looked disappointed. "Will there be a castle?" he asked.

"An inflatable kind," she said.

"Aw," Riley replied.

Sister Lucy picked up a clipboard. "Let's see. There will be a treasure hunt, a bake sale, a pie-eating contest, a 'best looking animal' contest, bingo, face-painting, a dunking booth—"

"What's a dunking booth?" asked a girl named Kate.

Sister Lucy said, "Someone sits on a seat over a tank of water. People take turns throwing balls at a target. If they hit the target, the person on the seat drops in."

"Who will sit on the seat?" asked Brad.

Sister Lucy smiled again. "I think Father Cliff said he'll take a turn."

Some of the kids chuckled at the thought.

"There will also be a slow-pitch softball tournament," she said.

Riley's hand shot up. "Softball wasn't invented until a long time after Robin Hood."

"You're probably right," Sister Lucy agreed. "I don't think they had inflatable castles either."

This got another laugh from the kids.

Sam looked over at her brother. He sat at his desk with a very serious look on his face. She wondered what was wrong with him.

"There will be raffles and prizes throughout the day," Sister Lucy concluded. "Think about the things you want to do. You'll need to sign up for the softball tournament and a few other things. I'll pass around the sheet."

"I wonder if they'll have catapults," Riley whispered to Sam.

Sam looked at him. She wasn't sure what he meant.

"To launch boulders when we storm the castle," Riley explained.

Sam rolled her eyes. "You are so strange," she said.

***

During recess, Riley and Brad tossed a softball back and forth. They didn't have their gloves so they threw underhand. Nick sat on a bench and watched them. He kept thinking about his throwing.

"Did you sign up for the softball game?" Brad asked Nick after tossing the ball to Riley.

Nick shook his head.

"Why not?" Brad asked.

Suddenly Riley pretended they were in a real baseball game and said, like an announcer, "Oh no, it's a grounder to center field! Nick Perry dashes in for the play!"

Riley threw the softball hard to the ground. It bounced to Nick. Nick leaned from the bench and scooped it up.

Brad moved back and called out, "He throws to second base!"

Nick stood up. He threw the softball overhand to Brad.

The ball went wide to the right, out

of Brad's reach.

Oh no, Nick thought and felt his cheeks flush with embarrassment.

The ball landed, bounced, and rolled near the swing set. Sam was there with Kim. She saw the ball and picked it up.

"Here," Sam said. She drew back her arm and sent the ball soaring to Brad.

Nick watched as the ball flew into Brad's cupped hands.

"That was a good throw," said Mr. Hildreth. He was one of the school's gym teachers. He was standing next to the double doors that led back into the school. He was a short, stocky man with a face like a bulldog and gray hair that was cut flat on top like an Army drill sergeant.

The gym teacher walked toward Brad. "Toss me the ball," he said.

Brad threw the ball to Mr. Hildreth.

"Move further back," Mr. Hildreth told him.

Brad backed up further into the open field that was part of the school grounds.

Mr. Hildreth strode over to Sam and handed the ball to her. "Throw it to him again."

Nick frowned. He knew what was going to happen.

Sam took the ball and threw it all the way to Brad. Brad took only a small step and caught it in his bare hands.

"Do you practice at home?" Mr. Hildreth asked Sam.

"No, sir," she replied.

"Sign up for the softball tournament. Your class needs you," he said.

Sam nodded.

Mr. Hildreth walked back to the door. He leaned against the wall and watched them.

Nick went back to the bench and sat down. Riley came over and sat next to him.

"That's awkward," Riley said.

Nick looked away without answering.

Brad ran up to them. "What are you doing? Let's play catch."

Riley gave a short chuckle. "Oh no. I don't want to look stupid in front of Mr. Hildreth."

"You mean, like I did," Nick said.

Riley gave him a slight shrug.

"You'll get better if you practice," Brad replied.

"We play catch all the time and I'm not getting better," Nick said.

"You can't give up," Brad replied.

Nick looked over at his sister. She was standing next to the swing set talking to Kim again. Then she glanced over at him, almost as if he'd called her name.

Nick looked away.

Giving up seemed like a really good idea to him.

CHAPTER THREE

— · —

Car Talk

"I don't want to talk about it," Nick said to Sam.

They stood outside of the school waiting for their mom to pick them up. Lizzy stood off to the side, huddled in a talk with two other girls from her class.

"Why not?" Sam asked. She had been worried about Nick ever since recess.

She saw the family minivan pull into the parking lot. Her father was driving. He pulled into a spot and opened the door. He waved to them.

Lizzy broke away from her friends and went to the crosswalk. Sam followed, with Nick trailing behind her. Andrew came running from the schoolyard. He got to the van first and jumped into the front passenger seat.

Mr. Perry opened the door to the back of the van.

"Where's Mom?" Sam asked her father.

"She was asked to help at the soup kitchen again," he said.

Sam's mom had been working as a volunteer at St. Clare's soup kitchen downtown since Advent. It seemed like she'd been there a lot lately.

Lizzy climbed in and made her way to the back seat. Sam and Nick sat in the middle seats. Mr. Perry slid the door closed and climbed into the driver's seat.

"How is everybody?" he asked as he began the drive home.

No one answered. Their dad looked at them in the rearview mirror.

"Go on, Nick," their father said. "How was your day?"

"Okay," he said in a low voice.

"Uh oh," Mr. Perry said. "What's going on?"

Andrew looked back at them from the front passenger seat. "Something happened at recess. Mr. Hildreth was impressed at Sam's throwing."

Nick glared at Andrew. "How do you know about that?"

Andrew said, "I saw him in the hall. He told me he saw Sam throw a ball at recess. He said she was good. He asked me why she doesn't play for any of the Little League teams."

"Mr. Hildreth complimented Sam?" their dad said, surprised. "He doesn't compliment anybody about anything."

Nick turned his gaze to the window. "I *really* don't want to talk about it," Nick said.

"It's not my fault," Sam said.

"I'm confused," Mr. Perry said. "What does Sam's throwing have to do with Nick?"

Andrew said, "Nick is bothered because Sam is better at throwing than he is."

Nick folded his arms and scowled. "It's not fair," he said. "I practice all the time and can't throw. Sam doesn't practice and it goes wherever she aims the ball."

"I don't know why," Sam said.

"Some people are gifted at certain things," Mr. Perry said. "Some people have to work hard to develop their skills."

"And some people are never good no matter what they do," Nick said.

"Is that what you think?" Mr. Perry asked Nick.

Nick pressed his lips together.

There was silence in the van for a few moments until Andrew asked, "If Mom is out, can we have pizza for dinner?"

***

The family sat down together, prayed for God to bless the food, and then began to eat their pizza.

"Your mother is helping at the soup kitchen more because some of the volunteers have left," their father explained.

"Why can't they get more help?" Lizzy asked.

"Father Cliff keeps asking people at the church to step up, but everyone seems so busy. I'll help when I can," he said.

"Can I help?" asked Lizzy.

"Not until school is finished," Mr. Perry said. He gazed at his children. "The move is going to put more pressure on all of us. We need to do our part, especially with packing."

"Do you want us to throw everything into the boxes?" Andrew asked.

"Wrap everything in the packing paper first," his father said.

"*Everything?*" Sam asked.

"Not everything," Mr. Perry said. "Pack only those things you actually use or that have personal value to you. Put everything else in the hall. Your mother and I will decide what to do with that stuff."

"It's going to get crazy," Andrew said as he peeled a slice of pepperoni off of his slice of pizza. He held it up, then tossed it into his mouth.

"We're going to discover all kinds of things under Nick's bed," Sam teased.

The family laughed. Nick didn't. He was hunched over his plate and had a sour look on his face.

"Nick," Mr. Perry said.

Nick looked up at him.

"We can go out back and practice throwing," his dad said.

Nick shook his head. "I have homework to do."

"You'd rather do homework than throw ball?" Andrew said. "Something's seriously wrong."

Sam looked at Nick. His forehead was bunched up into wrinkles.

She remembered how her grand-mother always said, "Be careful or your face might freeze like that." She opened her mouth to say it to him, then changed her mind. He wouldn't have thought it was funny.

CHAPTER FOUR

— · —

Paper Balls

After the dinner dishes were cleaned up, Nick went off to his room. He tried to tell himself that his throwing wasn't important. It didn't matter that Sam was better at it. But it kept nagging at him.

He paced around his room for a few minutes. He sat down at his desk to do his math homework. Then his eye went to a sheet of packing paper. He tore off a corner and crumpled it into a ball. Across the room was a poster of Frodo and Sam from *The Lord of the Rings*.

They were walking toward a mountain range. The highest peak was Mount Doom. It looked fuzzy in the distance.

Nick took aim at the top of Mount Doom and threw the ball of paper. It hit the wall to the right of the poster.

He tore off another piece of packing paper, crumpled it up, and tried again. This time the paper ball veered off to the left.

He tried again. The paper ball hit the bottom of the poster.

He tried again and the paper ball hit the middle of the poster.

"I can't be *that* bad," Nick said to himself.

He tore at another sheet of packing paper. More paper balls, more throws. But he couldn't hit the top of Mount Doom.

"What are you doing?" The question came from the doorway. His dad was standing there.

Nick blushed. "I was . . . practicing."

His dad pointed to the balls of paper on the floor. There must have been a couple of dozen scattered around like tumbleweeds. "With those?"

"Yeah," said Nick.

His dad moved into the room. "What were you trying to hit?"

Nick showed him Mount Doom on the poster.

"How did you do?" Mr. Perry asked.

"I couldn't hit it."

"Let's try again," said Mr. Perry.

Nick and his father picked up the balls of paper.

***

Sam was in her room trying to pack up a moving box. She picked up a doll that was her favorite a year ago. Now she hardly looked at it. First she put it in the "get rid of" pile, and then she put it in the "keep" pile. Then she put it back again.

Lizzy sat on the edge of Sam's bed and watched her sister. She looked like she might burst out laughing.

Sam picked up a small electronic dog with a speaker on its back. It used to wiggle and bark when music played.

"This was fun for about a week," she said. She put it in the "get rid of" pile.

"I thought you cleaned out all your stuff last year, when we moved from Denver," Lizzy said.

"I didn't want to get rid of anything then," Sam said. Now she wondered why she kept so many toys. "Looks like junk now."

"Mom and Dad would say there's a lesson in this," Lizzy said.

Sam held up a sketchbook filled with drawings she'd done. Some were done with crayons, some with pencil. "I can throw this away," she said.

"Wait," Lizzy said and held out her hand. "Let me see."

Sam gave her the sketchbook.

Lizzy flipped through the pages. "You should keep it."

"Why? They're terrible."

Lizzy held up one of the pages. "That's a good drawing of a horse."

"It's *purple*," Sam said.

Lizzy held up another. "This one looks like our neighbor's dog in Denver," she said.

Sam glanced at it and snorted. "That looks more like a horse than the drawing of the horse did."

Lizzy shrugged. "You have to start somewhere."

"You're the artist in the family," Sam said.

"A family can have more than one," said Lizzy.

"But I'll never be as good as you," Sam said.

Lizzy frowned at her. "You're not supposed to be as good as me. You're supposed to be as good as you."

Sam didn't see any point in arguing about it.

"Keep your sketchbook," Lizzy said. "One day you can look back and see how much better you got. That's why I keep all my old sketchbooks and writings."

The word "writings" made Sam think of letters, which caused her to think of Kim's letter from her parents, which led her to think about St. Paul's instruction to "rejoice always."

"Do you think Christians are supposed to rejoice all of the time?" Sam asked her sister.

Lizzy slid off of the bed. "That's a funny question. Why are you asking now?"

Sam explained about Kim's letter and the Bible verse.

"I think St. Paul wrote it kind of like when parents tell kids to eat all of their vegetables," Sam said.

Lizzy shook her head. "If St. Paul

said it, then he meant it."

"But what does it mean?" Sam asked. "How are we supposed to rejoice always? Are we supposed to be happy when bad things happen?"

Lizzy said, "Good things happen and bad things happen and we're supposed to rejoice because we remember that God loves us."

Suddenly there was a loud *thump* on the other side of the wall. Then came a crash.

"Uh oh," Lizzy said.

The girls sprinted next door to Nick's room.

The first thing Sam saw was Nick standing with his hand over his mouth. The second thing she saw was her dad picking up a lamp from the floor. The third thing was the floor with dozens and dozens of paper balls littered all over it.

"What's going on?" Sam asked.

Her father started to chuckle. Then Nick giggled. Soon, the two of them were laughing loud and hard.

Sam couldn't imagine what they'd been doing. She looked at Lizzy. "Do boys ever grow up?" she asked.

Lizzy smiled. "I hope not," she said.

Just then Sam's mom came up the stairs. She walked slowly and her eyes were narrow. She looked at the two girls. Then she looked into Nick's room and saw the balls of paper all over the floor.

She gave a little groan and said, "I'm going to bed."

***

"I never hit the top of Mount Doom," Nick said to his dad. They had just finished picking up the paper balls. Now they were kneeling on the floor, spreading the paper flat again.

"Yes, you did," Mr. Perry said.

"That didn't count," Nick said. "I had

my eyes closed."

His dad smiled. He pressed his hands down on the sheet of packing paper to iron the wrinkles out. Nick noticed that it didn't work.

"Why are we doing this?" Nick asked.

"So the paper is ready for you to use," his dad said. "We don't want to waste it."

"But it looks ruined," Nick said. Mr. Perry picked up a sheet. "Packing paper is made to be used over and over." He grabbed a book from Nick's desk and wrapped the paper around it. "See? The paper hugs the book. And

another sheet will protect it."

Nick had never really thought about the wonders of packing paper before. He figured it was the stuff the newspapers couldn't use for some reason.

His dad picked up another ball and un-crumpled it. He asked, "Nick, what's really bugging you? Is it that you want to be good at throwing or that Sam throws better than you?"

Nick thought about it, then said, "Both."

Mr. Perry pondered his son for a moment. "Sam may have a natural talent for aiming and throwing. Some people do. Just like some people can sing or dance or work with numbers or design buildings or write stories. They're born with it."

"What if you weren't born with any talent?" Nick asked.

"I believe most people are born with talents," his dad said, "but some haven't discovered what those talents are yet."

Nick picked up a paper ball. "What are they supposed to do in the meantime?"

"Develop their skills," his dad said.

Nick wasn't sure what he meant. "Isn't that the same thing?"

Mr. Perry got an *I-really-have-to-think-about-how-to-explain-it* look on his face. Then he said, "You're born with talent. But skills are what you do with your talent. Like, I might be good at designing a shirt, but I need sewing skills to make the shirt."

"Can you have skills without talent?" Nick asked.

"I think so," his dad said. "When I was younger, my parents made me learn to play piano. My fingers hit the keys in the right ways, but I didn't really have any talent as a musician. Anybody who ever heard me play knew it. Do you know what I mean?"

Nick gave that some thought. "I

think so."

"Most of us have to discover what our talents are," his dad said. "And then we have to develop our skills to make those talents work."

Once the packing paper was sorted out, Nick's dad hugged him goodnight and left the room. Nick brushed his teeth and got into his pajamas. As he crawled into bed, he thought more about talent and skills.

What if I don't have any talent or skills? he thought.

He fell asleep wondering, *What if I'm not good at anything at all?*

CHAPTER FIVE

—·—

Being Happy

Sam and Kim sat next to each other at a large table in Sister Cecilia's art class. Sam was drawing a picture of a rose. Kim was drawing a picture of a boat on a lake. Sam thought her picture of a rose looked mostly like a weird stick insect eating brussels sprouts. *I'll never be as good as Lizzy*, she thought.

A girl named Hannah sat across from them. She was painting with watercolors. Sam watched her dab her paintbrush into a cup of water and then onto a small tray of colors. Hannah moved the brush around and then pressed it against the thick paper.

Sam thought Hannah was painting a face. Or it might have been a bowling ball.

"I don't know what it means," Kim said softly to Sam.

Sam had told Kim what Lizzy said about being happy all of the time.

Kim asked, "Are we supposed to be happy all of the time because we know God loves us?"

"I guess so," Sam said. "How can we be sad when we know that?"

Kim leaned onto the table. She drew some lines on the water under the boat to make it look like splashing waves. "Okay. I'll try to be happy, no matter what."

Sam drew thorns on the stem of her rose. She thought about how beautiful roses were up top, but how they had thorns to protect them. She remembered pricking her finger on a thorn and how much it hurt.

She thought, *If I prick my finger now, am I supposed to be happy about it?*

Sam leaned back and looked at her picture. The rose now looked like a cactus eating brussels sprouts.

Sam glanced up in time to see Hannah reach toward the cup of water with her paintbrush. The brush hit the side of the cup and knocked it over. The water spilled across the table and onto Kim's drawing.

"Oh no!" Hannah cried out.

Kim snatched up her drawing, but it was too late. The water had soaked into the top half of the paper.

"I'm so sorry!" Hannah said to Kim.

Sister Cecilia rushed over with a roll of paper towels. "It's all right," she said. She began mopping up the water.

Kim stared at the limp, soggy drawing in her hands. The picture was ruined.

"Don't worry," Kim said, though her

eyes were wide and tearful. She forced a smile onto her lips. "It's okay."

Sam knew it wasn't.

Later, Sam was with Kim in the girls' bathroom. Kim had burst into tears. "That drawing was for my parents," she sobbed.

Sam put a hand on her shoulder. "You can draw them another one."

Kim looked at Sam. "I tried to be happy. Did you see? I tried to smile."

"I saw," Sam said. But she had a hard time believing that St. Paul expected people to smile at a time like that.

***

"You're not playing softball at the spring festival?" Brad asked Nick during recess.

Nick, Brad, and Riley had been kicking a soccer ball around.

"What's the point?" Nick said. "I'll look bad."

"We're in third grade," Riley said. "We *always* look bad."

Brad shot him a sharp look. "Maybe *you* do," he said.

"I can't throw," Nick grumbled.

"You need to practice more," Brad said.

"Practice doesn't help. I don't have any talent—or skill," Nick said, thinking of what his dad had said the night before. "I can't do anything."

"Yes, you can," Riley argued.

"Like what?" Nick asked.

Brad and Riley went quiet.

"See?" said Nick.

Brad said, "You have to be good at *something*. Nobody's good at nothing."

The three boys thought about that sentence and decided it made sense.

"You can run faster than me," Riley offered.

"So can everyone else," Brad said.

"Stop picking on me," Riley said.

"I'm not!"

The two boys got into an argument about whether Brad was picking on Riley or not.

Nick tried to ignore them. He kept trying to think of something he was good at. Nothing came to mind.

"You're good at getting in trouble," Brad said to Nick, trying to change the subject with Riley.

Nick glanced at him. "You're good at getting me in trouble."

Riley held up his hand. "I know. Let's go through a list."

"What kind of list?" Nick asked.

"Anything we can think of," Riley answered. He began: "Are you good at science?"

"No."

"Math?"

"No."

"Spelling?"

"No."

Brad asked, "Can you play an instrument?"

"No."

"Sing?" asked Riley.

"No."

"Art?"

"No."

"Computers?"

"No."

"Video games?"

Nick hesitated, then said, "A little."

"Basketball?" asked Brad.

"No."

"Tennis?"

"No."

"Soccer?"

"No."

Riley asked, "Cleaning things up?"

"No."

"How about money?"

"No."

"Fixing things?"

"No."

"Pouring cement?"

Nick looked at Riley. "What?"

"I said anything that comes to mind."

"This isn't helping me," said Nick.

"What about geography?" Brad asked.

"No."

"History?"

"No."

"Are you good with animals?" asked Riley.

"Not really."

"Reptiles? Insects?" asked Brad.

"No."

"How about designing stuff?"

"No."

"Studying rocks?"

"No."

"Nuclear physics?" Riley asked.

"I don't know what that is," Nick said.

"Neither do I," Riley said.

There was a long pause. Then Brad asked, "Can you stand on your head?"

Nick remembered the last time he tried. "No," he said.

"Can you touch your nose with your tongue?" Riley asked.

Nick looked at him. "I'm done talking about this," he said.

***

While Nick was outside with Brad and Riley, Sam and Kim went back to their classroom. Sister Lucy was standing at the board. She was writing down math problems for them to do when the class came back.

"I heard about your drawing," Sister Lucy said to Kim. "I'm sorry."

Kim nodded, but didn't say anything.

"We want to ask you about a Bible

verse," Sam said.

Sister Lucy waved for the girls to sit down on the nearest chairs. She pulled the chair from behind her desk and sat across from them. "Go ahead," she said.

Sam explained about the letter from Kim's parents and the Bible verse from St. Paul.

"That's Philippians chapter four, verse four," Sister Lucy said. "'Rejoice in the Lord always, again I say rejoice.'"

Kim said, "I want to learn how to be happy all the time. But I don't think I can."

"Do you know about Philippi?" Sister Lucy asked.

The girls said they didn't.

"It was a big city," Sister Lucy explained. "It had Romans and Greeks and Jews and a small church that St. Paul started. The Christians were treated badly by the people around them. They were poor. They suffered a lot."

Sam thought about being poor and suffering. *What did that church think when Paul told them to rejoice?* she wondered.

"Do you know where Paul was when he wrote the letter to the church in Philippi?" Sister Lucy asked.

The girls looked at each other. Neither one knew.

"St. Paul was in prison," Sister Lucy said. "He was put in jail because of his faith."

Kim's eyes widened. "Just like my parents!"

Sister Lucy nodded. "He was suffering when he told a suffering church to 'rejoice always.'"

"But *how* did he expect them to be happy all of the time?" asked Kim.

"Is that what he told them?" Sister Lucy asked. "Did he say to be happy all of the time?"

Again, the girls weren't sure what to say.

Sister Lucy smiled at them. "He said to *rejoice*."

"Isn't it the same thing?" Kim asked.

Sister Lucy shook her head. "Being happy is how joy sometimes shows itself. But being happy is a *feeling*."

The girls looked at Sister Lucy. Sam hoped she would explain more.

Sister Lucy continued, "No one can have one feeling all of the time. Have you ever tried to stay angry or excited or sad or surprised *all* day? You can't. Our feelings are supposed to change. If you had the same feeling all the time, you would go crazy. St. Paul didn't tell them to have a feeling all of the time."

"So what was he talking about?" Sam asked.

"Rejoicing comes from having joy in our hearts," Sister Lucy said. "Joy is a gift from God. He gives it to us through the Holy Spirit. Joy is something we have because we trust that God loves us no matter what happens."

Sam remembered Lizzy saying something just like that.

Sister Lucy said, "That's how St. Paul could tell us to rejoice all of the time. He wasn't happy about being in prison. He didn't laugh all the time. He felt sad and even lonely. But he had joy because he knew that being in prison was where God wanted him to be."

Sam knew Kim was thinking about her parents.

Sister Lucy added, "It's like love. We love, even when we don't *feel* love. We love, even when things go wrong. We love because God shares his love with us. Joy is the same kind of thing. Does that help?"

Kim nodded.

"Would you mind if we prayed for your parents?" Sister Lucy asked.

Kim said that would be nice. So they did.

CHAPTER SIX

—— • ——

Exitus

Mrs. Perry picked up the four Perry kids after school. Nick approached the van and could see his mom through the glass. He thought his mom look tired.

"Uncle Clark is at the house talking to your father about the move," Mrs. Perry announced to them. "I put your dinner in the refrigerator. It's a chicken casserole. Your dad will warm it up for you."

"Where will you be?" Andrew asked his mom.

"The soup kitchen," she said.

"Why are you there so much?" Sam asked.

"A lot of people travel to town because the weather has warmed up," Mrs. Perry said. "Some need our help. And we don't have enough volunteers to serve them all."

"I'll help," Lizzy said.

"Thank you. But we need grown-ups," Mrs. Perry said.

She drove into the driveway and let the kids out of the van. They waved to her as she backed out again. She drove back toward town.

"Why does Mom look so tired?" Nick asked Sam as they went into the house.

"*Why?*" Sam frowned at him. "Aren't you paying attention?"

"Yes!" he said. Then he asked, "Paying attention to what? What did I miss?"

Sam grunted at him and walked into the kitchen.

Nick dropped his backpack by the stairs and followed voices to the dining room. His dad and Uncle Clark were leaning over the dining table, looking at papers and maps.

Andrew had already joined them. "What are you looking at?" he asked.

Lizzy stepped in and hugged her father. Then she moved around to the end of the table. Sam came alongside her dad. He put his arm around her shoulders and gave her a quick squeeze.

Nick circled around to the other end of the table. His Uncle Clark put a big paw of a hand on his head and tousled his hair.

"We were just talking about a mystery," Mr. Perry said.

"What kind of mystery?" Andrew asked.

Uncle Clark nodded to the table. "You know we found a lot of important artifacts at the hotel site," he said.

Nick remembered that the diggers had unearthed pots and jars and boxes from a really old Spanish mission. His

uncle had built a large shelter over it so the experts could explore what else was buried there.

"We found journals from one of the priests talking about a shrine to Mary in the forest, somewhere further up the mountain."

"Why is that a mystery?" asked Nick.

"Because we can't find it," said Uncle Clark.

"Maybe it was buried, like the mission," Lizzy suggested.

"That's what we thought," said Uncle Clark. "But Mrs. Ross at the church said she's been there. However, when she tried to lead us to it, she got lost."

Their dad said, "Other people claim they've seen it in the past twenty years. Some townspeople say they've had friends or relatives go there."

"I remember hearing about it when I was little," Mr. Perry said. "It's called the Shrine of Exitus. '*Exitus*' is Latin for a disappearance, a departure."

"Like 'exit,'" said Nick.

"That's right," his father said. "Local legends say that the shrine would appear to some people and then disappear without a trace."

"Like Big Foot," Nick threw out.

"Sort of," said his father.

Uncle Clark said, "The experts said that the letter from the mission site is the oldest reference to the shrine they have ever seen."

Andrew climbed onto a chair, his elbows on the table. He pushed close to a map. "Where is it supposed to be?"

The map looked like nothing but squares and squiggly lines to Nick.

Uncle Clark pointed to a squiggly line. "Along this trail," he said. "The experts have been all over that area. I went with them a few times. We can't find it."

Nick felt goosebumps on his arm.

"I read something about it," Andrew said.

All eyes went to him.

Andrew looked surprised to be the center of attention. "It was in a book about the history of Hope Springs. Alfred Virtue saw the shrine. So did Theodore Perry."

Alfred Virtue was an important leader of the town a hundred years ago, Nick remembered. He was also good friends with their ancestor Theodore Perry.

Mr. Perry's eyebrows shot up. "Ted Perry saw it? I've never heard that."

Andrew said, "It's what the book said."

"Show me," Uncle Clark said.

"It's at the library," Andrew said.

"Andrew spends all his time at the library now," Sam teased. "He goes with some girl he met. But he won't tell anyone about her."

"Her name's Eva and I don't meet her at the library," Andrew explained. "She helps her aunt at the Curiosity Shoppe. She's interested in history like I am."

Everyone's attention went back to the maps on the table.

"What a strange mystery," Mr. Perry said.

"Maybe it's a miracle," said Lizzy.

CHAPTER SEVEN

—.—

Discovery

The evening was filled with homework and more packing. Nick got tired of both and went into the family room to watch television. There was nothing on that he cared about.

Magazines and books were spread on the coffee table next to the couch.

Mom has been too busy to tidy up, Nick thought. Then he got the idea that he could do it. He picked up the books and put them on a shelf near the television. Then he began to sort through the magazines.

One of the magazines was for business people. *It must be one of Dad's,* Nick thought. A headline on the cover said, "How to Discover Your Talents!"

Nick opened the magazine and flipped through the pages to find a table of contents. Then he found the article. He turned to the page.

The article was written for grown-ups. But it had a page of multiple-choice questions that were supposed to help readers find their talents.

Nick looked at the first question. It asked: "The people closest to you would say you are . . .

   a. Funny

   b. Creative

   c. Wise

   d. Hardworking

   e. Helpful

   f. A risk-taker

   g. Smart

Nick looked over the list. He decided on "e" because he was tidying up without anyone telling him to do it. Or maybe it was "f" because he was taking a risk answering this quiz.

The next question asked: "How do you learn?

   a. By seeing

   b. By hearing

   c. By acting things out

   d. By working with my hands

   e. All of the above

Nick thought "e" because he couldn't imagine learning anything without "a" through "d."

Nick wondered what the first question had to do with the second. Then he saw that there were ten more questions to answer. One asked how he spent his time. Another asked if he's easily distracted.

He groaned. He didn't think a magazine quiz could be so hard. He tossed the magazine aside. *I'll do it later*, he decided.

He found a book filled with puzzles. It had crosswords and find-the-words and connect-the-dots and little quizzes. Most of the puzzles were filled out with pencil. Nick flipped the pages and stopped on a maze. No pencil markings.

He leaned over the book and put his finger on the start of the maze. Then he traced along the path and came to a dead end. He growled. He went to the start of the maze again and tried another path.

Another dead end. He started again and followed a path into the middle of the maze. He came to another dead end.

This is just like my life, he thought and tossed the book onto the table. *I can't do anything.*

A sharp laugh came from the door. It was Andrew.

"What's so funny?" Nick asked.

"Watching you do that puzzle," Andrew said.

Nick scowled at him. He wasn't in the mood to be teased. "Can *you* do it?"

"Not without a pencil," Andrew said. "I always get stuck, too."

He walked over to the coffee table and looked down. "Where's my book?" he asked.

"What book?"

"A book about the Rocky Mountains." Andrew waved at the table. "It was right here."

"Oh," Nick said. "Maybe I picked it

up. Look on the shelf. There, next to the TV."

Andrew went to the bookcase next to the TV. "Where?"

Nick pointed again. "Next to the big yellow book that says 'Pick Parks.'"

Andrew looked at the big yellow book, then back at Nick. "What did you say it's called?"

"*Pick Parks*," Nick said impatiently. "It's the one about National Parks. Mom and Dad bought it for our camping trip."

Andrew held a finger next to the yellow book. "Read that title to me."

Nick glared at his brother. "What's wrong with you? It's called *Pick Parks*!"

Andrew pointed at the words on the spine of the book. "It's called *Pikes Peak*."

Nick squinted his eyes and looked again. "Are you crazy? It says—"

"Look." Andrew pulled the yellow

book from the shelf. He carried it over to Nick. "See?"

Nick saw in big black letters the words "Pikes Peak."

He looked cross at Andrew. "I was wrong. Big deal."

Andrew went back to the bookshelf. He pointed to another large book with big print. "What does this one say?"

Nick looked. The words were a little fuzzy. He said slowly, "*Word Ex-plan-nations.*"

"It's called *World Explorations*," Andrew said. He pointed to a book on a different shelf. "What's the title of that one?"

Nick looked. The words were even fuzzier. "What's your point?" he asked.

***

Mrs. Perry came home around eight o'clock. Sam could hear her moving around in the kitchen. The *chink* of a plate on the counter, the *beep* of the microwave.

Sam guessed she was warming up the leftover chicken casserole.

Sam ran to her desk and grabbed a sign-up form for the spring festival. There were booths and tables to work, games to lead, and food to serve. The form was to get parents to help.

Sam's mom sat at the kitchen table. Sam saw lines around her eyes.

"Hi," she said. Her mouth usually settled into a slight smile. Now it seemed pulled down at the corners.

Lizzy walked in. She took a look at her mother and then looked at Sam.

The two girls exchanged a knowing look. They were both worried.

Sam jumped onto a chair on one side of her mother while Lizzy slid into the chair on the other side.

"Are you all right?" Lizzy asked.

"I'm tired," her mom said. She jabbed her fork at the plate of chicken.

Sam put the form on the table but

didn't say anything about it.

"What's that?" Mrs. Perry asked.

"This is for the spring festival," Sam said. "But Dad can look it over."

"Let me see," Mrs. Perry said.

"You don't have to," Sam said quickly. She felt bad for bringing the form at all.

"Leave it with me," she said.

The girls looked at each other.

"How was your week?" their mom asked.

Sam said, "Kim got a letter from her parents."

Mrs. Perry tipped her head a little. "Are they still in prison?"

"Uh huh. But Kim's mom is sick," said Sam.

"I'm sorry to hear that." Her mom jabbed a piece of chicken.

Sam told her about the "rejoice always" talks she'd been having. Sam explained what Sister Lucy had said about joy.

Mrs. Perry put her fork down. "Joy," she said softly. She gave a little shrug of her shoulders. "Maybe that's why I feel so tired."

"Why?" Lizzy asked.

Her mom said, "Sometimes we get so busy that we forget about *why* we're so busy."

"Are you talking about the soup kitchen?" Lizzy asked.

Mrs. Perry nodded. "Sometimes the people who come in need more help than we can give them. We don't have the staff. It wears me out."

"What can we do about it?" Sam asked.

"Pray for help," her mom replied. "And hope that others will volunteer."

"Can we help?" Lizzy asked.

Mrs. Perry touched Lizzy's arm. "Do what you can with school and packing. That helps me."

"I have an idea," Lizzy said. "Let's go

on a hike together."

Mrs. Perry looked at her as if a hike was the last thing she'd ever have time to do.

"We can look for the shrine," Lizzy added.

"That'd be fun!" Sam said.

"What shrine?" Mrs. Perry asked.

Lizzy told her about the mysterious shrine somewhere in the mountains. "Maybe we can find it. It might help you find joy," Lizzy concluded.

Her mother nodded and said, "Maybe so. We'll go one Saturday morning."

Mr. Perry walked into the kitchen. He smiled at his wife. "I'm glad you're home," he said.

"Why? What's wrong?" she asked.

Mr. Perry chuckled. "Nothing. I'm just glad you're home."

Mrs. Perry looked relieved.

"Though," Mr. Perry started to say and let the sentence hang in the air.

The three ladies at the table looked up at him.

"Nick needs glasses," he said.

——— . ———

CHAPTER EIGHT

Seeing Things

Sam and Kim were walking to class after the morning assembly. Sam saw Mr. Norm, the school handyman, cleaning the big aquarium near the school office.

"I want to look," Kim said, and the two girls stepped out of the flow of students to see him.

The tank had goldfish and guppies and one that was blue and silver and another that looked like a rainbow. There were blue rocks on the bottom with green plants sticking out. There was also a little castle and a sunken pirate ship and a couple of caves the fish darted in and out of. A filter hung over the side into the water and buzzed softly.

"Good morning," Mr. Norm said. He was wearing his overalls, and his sleeves were rolled up. He had the lid off of the top of the aquarium and was using a net to clean out some of the mess the fish had made. He also had a small tube. Sam had seen it before. It was like a vacuum that sucked up the muck on the bottom.

The girls moved in closer to see the fish. They were swimming this way and that.

"I've been thinking," Mr. Norm said. He had a toothpick tucked in the corner of his mouth. It wiggled up and down when he talked.

"About what?" asked Sam.

"The way these fish see the world," he said.

"What do you mean?" Kim asked.

He said, "I mean, they're swimming around, going about their business. They go down to the bottom and in and out of the little castle and caves. It's the only world they know." He lifted up the net and then gave it a *swish* in a bucket at his feet.

Sam wondered what Mr. Norm was talking about. It was hard to tell with him.

Mr. Norm stood up straight and eyed the tank. "What do they think when I show up?" he asked. "Am I a friend or an invader who has come to attack their world? Do they realize I'm the one giving them food and cleaning everything up or are they afraid I've come to ruin their lives? Are they relieved after I go away or are they happy that I came?"

Sam had never really thought about it.

"I think about how much they're like us," he said.

"You think we're like fish?" Kim asked.

He took the toothpick from one side of his mouth and tucked it in the corner of the other side. "Well," he said, "we're in our little worlds, going on about our lives. And we have no idea that there's a much bigger world just above the water line or on the other side of the glass. We don't realize all the ways that someone is taking care of us. And sometimes we think that his care is really trouble or an attack."

Sam smiled. She didn't realize cleaning a fish tank could be such a thoughtful job.

"It's all about our viewpoint," he said.

"We have to go to class," Kim said and tugged at Sam's sleeve.

Sam hesitated. "Do you think fish have joy?" she asked Mr. Norm.

He made a humming kind of noise

and then said, "I guess they have something like a fish-kind-of-joy when the water is just right and they've been fed and there's nothing to scare them. But I don't think they can have the kind of joy like we have. Our joy comes from knowing something they don't know."

"What?" Kim asked.

He pointed upward.

"A roof over their heads?" Sam teased.

He laughed. Then he turned back to the tank. "We're special in all of creation," he said. "A fish doesn't know that there's a huge world outside of their world. But God put it into us to believe that there is. It's like we have a nagging feeling about it. We're aware of God in a way that nothing else in all the world can be."

Kim pulled at Sam's arm.

"Thanks, Mr. Norm," Sam said as they headed down the hall for class.

He tipped a hand at them, like a salute.

Sam looked around her as she rushed to class. The walls of the school, the ceiling, the windows, and the classroom doors all seemed like a fish tank to her.

There's a whole world out there that I can't see, she thought.

The idea gave her goosebumps and a tingling in her stomach. She wondered if it was joy.

CHAPTER NINE

—•—

Near and Far

"Well, it's not so bad," Dr. Sydd said to Nick and his mother.

Dr. Sydd was an eye doctor. She was young and seemed to smile a lot. She told Nick to think of the eye tests like a game—looking into a machine and catching sight of the squiggly lines around the screen, or looking at letters on the wall through different lenses.

Nick's mom stood off to the side and watched it all quietly. But now she asked,

"What's not so bad?"

"Nick is nearsighted," Dr. Sydd replied, then she turned to Nick. "Your vision is good for reading and anything else up close. But your eyes are changing and you're not seeing distances so well."

Nick was still sitting in the patient's chair. "I didn't know until now."

"You didn't notice that Sister Lucy's writing on the blackboard was fuzzy?" Nick's mom asked.

Nick shook his head. "I thought she had fuzzy handwriting," he said.

Dr. Sydd smiled at him. "Sometimes you don't know that what you're seeing isn't as clear as it should be."

"Does he need glasses?" Mrs. Perry asked.

"Yes. I've written up the prescription."

"I'm going to have to wear *glasses*?" Nick asked. "Can I have the kind that'll let me see other worlds or change the

color of everything or show me the answers to tests?"

Mrs. Perry was aghast. "What have you been watching?" she asked him.

"These will help you to see *your* world," the doctor said.

"Will I be better at throwing?" Nick asked.

Dr. Sydd said, "Glasses won't help your throwing arm, but you'll be able to see what you're throwing at."

Nick suddenly had a surge of hope. Maybe he wasn't so bad at baseball after all.

Dr. Sydd turned to Nick's mom. "When's the last time you had your eyes checked?" she asked.

"I can't remember," was the answer.

"Your eyes look red. Are they irritated? Are you having headaches?" the doctor asked.

"Sometimes," said Mrs. Perry.

Dr. Sydd scooted Nick out of the

chair. "Sit down," she told his mom.

At the end of the appointment, both Nick and his mom had to choose frames for their new glasses.

"We'll have them within a week," Dr. Sydd said as they left.

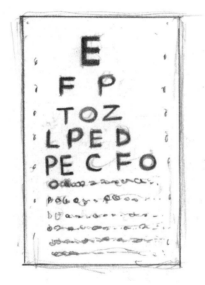

Mrs. Perry dropped Nick off at school and signed him in at the office. Nick was just in time for the third-grade gym class.

The students were spread into a wide circle playing "dodge" with a large ball made of some kind of sponge.

Nick walked over to Mr. Hildreth. He was standing off to the side watching the kids play. He had a sour look on his face, like he'd just swallowed a bug.

"Where've you been?" Mr. Hildreth asked.

"I had a doctor's appointment," Nick said. He pointed at the game. "Do you want me to play?"

Mr. Hildreth shook his head. "No. The sides are even."

Nick watched the game. It looked like the teams were divided between the two third-grade classes. Nick's class formed the circle. The other class was inside the circle, dodging the ball.

Mr. Hildreth frowned. He said to Nick, "When I was your age, we played dodgeball with a *real* ball."

Nick had heard his dad talk about

those days. "You threw a soccer ball at each other?"

"That's right," said Mr. Hildreth.

"Didn't it hurt?" asked Nick.

"You bet it did," Mr. Hildreth said. "There's no replacing black eyes, broken fingers, and fractured ribs for building character."

Nick couldn't tell if he was joking or not.

The ball sailed past a boy inside the circle and straight into Sam's arms. She quickly threw it again and hit one of the girls.

"You're out!" Mr. Hildreth shouted.

The girl unhappily stomped her feet and came out of the game.

"What's your sister's name?" Mr. Hildreth asked.

"Samantha. But we call her Sam."

"Samantha Perry!" Mr. Hildreth called out. He strode forward and broke through the circle to the middle.

The game came to a halt as all of the kids turned.

Sam raised her hand.

"Give me the ball," Mr. Hildreth said to Brad, who was getting ready to throw.

Brad tossed him the ball. Brad looked at Nick. Nick rolled his eyes.

Mr. Hildreth walked the ball over to Sam and handed it to her. "Throw it again," he said and moved out of the way.

The kids inside the circle were confused about what to do.

"Go on," he said to them. "It's *dodgeball*, so *dodge the ball!*"

The game resumed. Nick watched as Sam looked at a boy to the left. Then she suddenly threw the ball to the right and hit a different boy.

Mr. Hildreth laughed. "Nice trick," he said to Sam. He grabbed the ball again and tossed it back to her.

"Aren't we going to throw?" a boy named David May asked from the other side of the circle.

"We'll see," said Mr. Hildreth. Then he said to Sam, "Go."

The game started up again. The kids inside the circle moved this way and that to stay clear of Sam's throw. Her eyes darted back and forth. Then she threw fast and hard. The ball hit a boy near the far edge of the group.

"Did you sign up for the spring festival softball tournament?" Mr. Hildreth asked Sam.

"No, sir," she said.

"Why not?"

"I don't like to play baseball," she replied.

"With that arm, you should learn to like it," he said. "I want you to sign up."

She said, "But I—"

Mr. Hildreth already turned away from her and blew his whistle. "That's all!" he shouted.

It was a mystery to Nick where the whistle came from or how he got it into his mouth so fast.

The kids scattered to go back to their classes.

Sam walked over to Nick. She looked bothered. "I don't want to play," she whispered.

Nick grunted and said, "At least he wants you in the game. He doesn't care if I play or not."

Sam frowned. "What am I supposed to do?" she asked.

Nick gave her a hard look. "You can't say no to Mr. Hildreth. You have to sign up for the tournament."

***

That night, Sam told her dad about what had happened with Mr. Hildreth.

"You don't have to sign up for the tournament if you don't want to," said her father.

"But Mr. Hildreth will nag me about it," Sam said.

"Just tell him no. Be firm," her dad said.

"*You* should tell him."

"*Me*?" Her dad shook his head. "He scares the living daylights out of me."

"Dad!" Sam cried out.

Her dad laughed. "Calm down. It'll be okay."

Sam sighed with relief.

Then he said, "I'll ask your mother to talk to him."

Sam glared at her father. "You're joking, right? Is that a joke?"

Her dad grinned.

CHAPTER TEN

—— • ——

In Focus, Out of Control

"Dad! There's Mr. Hildreth!" Sam said as the Perry family van pulled into the school parking lot.

"What? Where?" her dad asked.

"Over there. By the front door. You can talk to him about the tournament," said Sam.

Mr. Perry pulled into a parking spot. He looked toward the school and said, "He's doing the car pool this morning. I shouldn't distract him."

"Don't be a scaredy-cat," Sam said.

Her dad turned off the engine, undid his seatbelt, and opened the door. "If I'm not back in five minutes, call the police." He slipped out.

The kids watched their dad walk across the lot to the school.

Andrew asked, "Why does Dad need to talk to Mr. Hildreth?"

Sam explained, "Dad's going to tell him that I don't want to play in the spring festival softball tournament."

"Why don't you want to play?" Nick asked. "Is it because of me? Look, I don't care if you can throw better than I can."

"Really?" Sam asked.

"Don't worry about it," he said. "I took a magazine quiz that said I have all the talent I need to become an office worker."

"What kind of office worker?" Lizzy asked from the back of the van.

"I don't know," Nick said. "There was

a picture of a guy with a white shirt and a tie. I guess I'll be like him."

Sam turned to her brother. "I don't want to play because I don't want to play."

Their father had crossed to where Mr. Hildreth stood.

"Is Dad afraid of Mr. Hildreth?" Lizzy asked.

"Isn't everybody?" asked Andrew.

Mr. Perry walked over to the gym teacher. He said something. Then Mr. Hildreth said something with a pointed finger. And something else. And something else. And then Mr. Perry nodded and made his way back to the van.

He opened the driver's door and looked surprised to see the kids waiting there. "I was only joking about waiting here. You should go inside." Then he looked alarmed. "You didn't call the police, did you?"

The kids laughed. Their father sat down behind the wheel.

"Well? What happened?" Sam asked.

"It was simple," Mr. Perry said. "I told him you have a rare medical condition and if you played softball your arm would fall off."

The kids screeched.

"You did not!" Sam said. "What did you *really* tell him?"

"I told him you don't want to play," her father stated.

"*And?*" asked Sam.

Mr. Perry turned in the seat to face her. "And he said that if I were a better parent I'd *make* you play. Otherwise you'll never be good at anything in life."

The kids looked at him, stunned.

"Wow," said Andrew. "What did you say to that?"

"I said I was willing to take that chance." Mr. Perry gazed at Sam. "So now you have to become a Mother Teresa or cure cancer to prove him wrong. No pressure, though."

He smiled at her.

Sam slumped back in her seat. "Maybe I should sign up for the tournament."

Mr. Perry reached back and patted her leg. "It's entirely up to you."

***

Nick was sitting with Brad and Riley at lunch. He told them about the magazine quiz.

"You *can't* be an office worker," Riley was saying while he loudly chewed his peanut butter and jelly sandwich. "Kids our age want to be firemen and astronauts and lion-tamers. *Not* office workers."

"I'm just telling you what the quiz said," said Nick. He was eyeing his plastic container. It had a small cluster of carrot pieces in the bottom. "Mom usually cuts these into strips so I can pick them up with my fingers."

"Who cut those?" Brad asked.

"My dad. He's been trying to help Mom at home because she's been so busy." Nick tried to pick up the pieces with his fingers. They were squishy.

Brad licked off a fork. "Here. You can use this."

"No thanks," Nick said. He went over to the baskets of silverware and got a spoon. When he sat down again, he said, "I hope my new glasses will help."

"Glasses won't tell you what to do with your life," Riley said.

Brad sipped his drink. The carton gurgled loudly as he finished it. "My dad says that men who don't know what to do with their lives become priests," he said.

"That's not true," Nick said.

"I think he's trying to be funny," said Brad.

"Does anyone laugh?" Riley asked.

"No." Brad dropped the carton onto the table. "My mom won't speak to him when he says things like that."

The two boys looked at him.

"Why not?" Nick asked.

"Her brother is a priest." Brad thought about it for a moment. "Her uncle is a priest, too. So is her cousin. In fact, I think she comes from a whole family of priests. I heard her tell my dad that she sometimes wishes she'd become a nun. But that's usually after we leave clothes lying around the house."

Riley said, "Being a priest isn't a normal job. They're *called* by God to be priests. They don't need things like talent or skill."

"That's crazy," Nick said. "They need *a lot* of talent and skill to do what they do."

"Maybe God is calling *you* to be a priest," Brad suggested.

Nick's mouth fell open. He hadn't thought of that. "How am I supposed to know?"

"You should ask Father Cliff," Riley said.

Nick got butterflies in his stomach. "What am I supposed to say? 'Hi, Father Cliff. I'm no good at throwing a baseball, so I think God wants me to be a priest.' That's silly."

A rascally smile formed on Brad's face. "You can ask him now. He's right over there."

Nick looked. Father Cliff was talking to another table of students.

"No," Nick said, but it was too late. Brad was on his feet and calling out to Father Cliff.

Father Cliff saw him, waved, said something to the other table, and then walked over.

Nick lowered his head. *How can God call me to be a priest when Brad is driving me crazy?* he thought.

"Hi, boys," Father Cliff said. Father Cliff was young and easy-going. He had dark hair and some of the girls said he was handsome like a movie star. Nick was impressed because he liked sports. "What's going on?"

"Nick was wondering how you know if God is calling you to be a priest," Brad said.

Father Cliff gazed at Nick. "That's not a question with a quick answer. If you're serious, we can talk about it. Are you serious?"

Nick looked up at him. "I don't know. We were just talking, and Brad brought it up."

"Oh," said Father Cliff. "Then maybe *Brad* is being called to the priesthood."

Brad nearly fell off of his chair. "Not me! Collars make my neck itch."

Father Cliff laughed. Then he said, "It's always a good idea to keep your ears open to God's call. He may not ask you to become priests, but he calls us all to serve him in one way or another. You should pray and ask him."

Father Cliff moved away to another table.

Nick hadn't thought about praying to find out what his talents are. "I *should* pray," he told Riley. Then he said to Brad, "And *you* should pray that I don't hurt you for making a scene."

Brad chuckled.

Nick didn't.

CHAPTER ELEVEN

——•——

Seeing Clearly

Nick was surprised at the end of the school day when his mother and father showed up in two different cars.

"You're coming with me," his mother said. "Our glasses are here."

They drove to Dr. Sydd's office. The nurse at the front desk took them to a side room and brought their glasses in on a couple of small trays.

"Let's try them on," the nurse said.

She handed Nick his new glasses. He held them carefully. He was afraid of dropping them. Then he slipped them on. His mom did the same with her glasses. They looked at each other and smiled.

"You look like a librarian," he said to her.

"You look like a professor," she said to him.

Nick looked around. "Everything looks the same." He felt a little disappointed.

"They're for distances," the nurse explained. "Go to the window and look out. First without your glasses, then look with them.

Nick did as she said. He looked out of the window without his glasses. He could see the building across the street. It was a clothes shop. He could see the front glass door and the big display window and the clothes on the mannequins. One wore a red dress, another wore a blue skirt and green top, while another wore a long dark coat.

Then he put on his glasses. He gasped. He saw the clothes shop again, but now he saw a sign posted on the front glass door. The sign gave the hours for the shop. And the clothes in the display window suddenly had details he didn't see before. The red dress had thin gold lines around the collar and along the sleeves. The blue skirt had green woven into it. The long dark coat was black with dark blue buttons. He could even see the lining around the pockets on the coat.

"Good?" his mom asked.

"This is amazing," he nearly shouted. "I feel like Superman!"

He craned his head to look up and down the street. The colors seemed brighter on the cars at the stoplight and on the signs hanging over the stores. The brick and stone of the buildings had deep lines. Even the parking meters along the sidewalk seemed dazzling.

"I can see *everything* now," he said.

His mom and the nurse chuckled behind him.

He flexed his arm. He couldn't wait to get home to practice his throwing.

***

The first thing he did when he got home was to grab Andrew for a game of catch. The boys grabbed their gloves and went into the backyard.

"Nice glasses," Andrew said as he tossed Nick the ball.

They spread out to each end of the large green rectangle that served as the yard.

Nick marveled that Andrew looked so clear to him at that distance.

Andrew pounded his glove and held it up. "Okay, let's go."

This is the test, Nick thought. He wound up and threw the ball. It flew to the right of Andrew and down sharply to the ground.

Nick growled.

"It's all right," Andrew said and retrieved the ball. He threw it back. "Try again."

Nick looked carefully at Andrew's glove. He wound up and threw.

The ball sailed to the right again, over Andrew's head.

Nick felt disappointed and could feel his disappointment turn into anger somewhere inside of him.

"Stay calm," Andrew called to him.

"I know that," Nick snapped.

More throws back and forth. Each time Andrew had to scramble to reach for the ball, narrowly catching it in his glove or having to chase it.

Nick fumed. Why couldn't he throw better now that he could see? What was wrong with him?

"You're throwing wild. It's about aim and control," Andrew said.

"*I know!*" Nick cried out. He was in a blind rage now. He took aim again and threw the ball with all of his might. The ball veered to the left. Andrew threw himself at it with his arm and glove outstretched.

The ball hit the tip of Andrew's glove and rebounded sharply toward the house.

Nick watched it with growing horror. The ball seemed to fly in slow motion. It flew past the barbecue and the short wooden stairs leading up to the back of the house—and then crashed straight through a small pane of glass on the back door.

Andrew, who had fallen to the ground, got to his feet.

Nick felt his legs go wobbly.

His dad's face appeared in the place where the pane of glass had been. "I hope you weren't *trying* to do that," he said.

***

The Perry family had a rule about understandable accidents versus reckless accidents. They both happen, Nick knew, but reckless accidents deserved some sort of punishment.

"Can we pretend like you've already yelled at me, since I feel really bad already?" Nick asked.

His dad nodded. "This was an understandable accident," he announced.

They cleaned up the glass just inside of the door.

"We have to work on your throwing some more," his dad said.

"It's no good," Nick said. He felt like crying now. "I can't throw! I can't do *anything*! Even with my new glasses!"

"You have plenty of time to figure out what your talents and skills are," his father said.

"It won't take any time, because I don't have any," said Nick.

Mr. Perry took his son by the shoulders and led him over to a kitchen chair. He knelt down to look Nick in the eyes. "Listen to me. That's *not* true. There may be a lot of reasons why you aren't very good at throwing. You're growing. Your body is changing. You need to develop your coordination. Those things take time."

Nick's whole body drooped. He fought the tears that came to his eyes behind his new glasses.

"Go up to your room and cool down," his dad said.

Nick jumped off of the chair and raced away. He nearly knocked Andrew over at the bottom of the stairs.

Andrew started to say, "It's not as bad as—"

But Nick wasn't listening. He dashed into his room and pushed the door closed behind him. He dove onto his bed. With a sob, he pressed his face into his pillow.

CHAPTER TWELVE

—— • ——

A New View

Sam and Lizzy declared Saturday the "Give Mom a Break" day. It began with Mr. Perry, Lizzy, and Sam serving her breakfast in bed while Andrew and Nick tidied up the main family areas.

"It's like the Mother's Day we didn't have because of your First Communion," Lizzy said to Sam.

After that breakfast, the Perry girls got ready for a hike along the trail where the mysterious Shrine of Exitus had been seen by various people at various times. The two girls put sandwiches, snacks, and bottled water into their backpacks.

Mrs. Perry drove up into the mountain and past the still-growing hotel that Uncle Clark was building. They reached the trailhead for the path marked on the map and parked. It was a beautifully sunny day with pale blue skies. A couple of fat, lazy clouds slowly drifted along.

They hardly spoke as they walked. Sam figured that was because of the silent beauty around them. There was only the soft crunch of pine needles and dirt on the trail beneath their feet. To the left and right the birds sang and some darted between the pine and aspen and maple trees. Sam watched shrubs of juniper and pink wild rose bushes shiver from animals unseen. And the sagebrush spread everywhere.

"If we follow this all the way up, we'll come to a cliff that overlooks Hope Springs," Lizzy said.

The three of them trekked on. Sam lost track of how long they had been walking or how far they'd gone. Looking ahead, she could see a gap in the trees and a shaft of golden light. They picked up their pace and soon came to a small meadow with green grass and tall willows. It led to another patch of pine trees and then the end of the trail.

Sam gasped. Spread out before them was the vast valley that housed the town of Hope Springs. The town looked like an island surrounded by fields and hills, ranches and farms. A river cut through the scene and then disappeared into the landscape. Sam's eyes went to the downtown area with the clock tower in the City Hall and the shops, and there, a little to the left, was

the Old Perry House and St. Clare's. Further on was the neighborhood where they now lived.

Sam heard a sniffle and looked up at her mom. Tears streamed down her face.

"What's wrong?" Sam asked.

The girls came in close. Mrs. Perry hugged them, then pointed toward the town. "There's the soup kitchen. It's that red-looking building."

The tears started to fall again.

"Why does it make you cry?" Lizzy asked.

Her mom pulled a tissue from her pocket and dabbed at her eyes. "When I'm there," she said, "everything seems so *big*—all the problems and the work and the responsibilities. But when I stand up here, it seems small, almost like a piece to a beautiful puzzle."

Sam looked at the town and wondered if this is how God sees things.

Mrs. Perry sniffled again and gave the

girls another hug. "Thank you for doing this," she said. "Sometimes it helps to get a different view of the world."

The three of them shrugged off their backpacks and sat down right where they were for a picnic. Sam thought the sandwiches tasted better and the water tasted fresher than she'd ever known.

Suddenly Mrs. Perry held her hands up and whispered, "Look."

Sam and Lizzy turned. Back in the meadow stood a herd of mule deer. They were brown and white and walked slowly across the grass. Then one with giant antlers stopped to look at the girls. The rest of the herd did the same.

Sam gave them a little wave. Then the deer walked on and disappeared into the thicket.

A little while later, they put on their backpacks again and made their way back to the trail. They hadn't gone far when Lizzy suddenly stopped.

"Do you hear that?" she asked.

Sam and her mom listened. All was silent.

"It sounded like a woman was laughing," Lizzy said. She turned to their right and looked at the woods.

They listened again. Sam couldn't hear anything.

Lizzy tilted her head. "There. Can't you hear it? A woman is laughing and . . . a baby. It's giggling. Like it's being tickled."

Sam and her mom looked at each other. Sam's mom shook her head. "I don't hear it."

"That way," Lizzy said and pointed.

Sam's mother looked down at the ground. "I didn't notice that before." She pointed to an overgrown path that stretched away from the main trail.

"Can we follow it?" Lizzy asked. Her eyes were wide and her face seemed radiant.

"Let's have an adventure," Mrs. Perry said.

They walked down the path and into the deepest and darkest forest Sam had ever seen. The air was thick with the smell of pine. Sam looked at the dull gray light to the left and right. She wondered if the floor of the forest had ever felt the full touch of sunlight.

"We're not walking on dirt," Mrs. Perry said.

The three of them stopped and looked down. The path was made of flat stones.

"Somebody put these here," Sam said. A tingling feeling touched the back of her neck and made goosebumps on her arms.

Lizzy softly said, "Ah," and looked ahead as if she'd heard the sound of a woman and baby laughing again. They pressed onward.

"How far should we go?" Sam asked.

"This path could go for miles."

"Don't worry," Lizzy said. "It's just up ahead."

"What is?" her mother asked.

"The Shrine," said Lizzy.

They didn't walk much further when they came to a small clearing. It was as if the trees had stepped aside to make way for a special guest. Beams of golden sunlight came down like spotlights on the clearing.

Lizzy suddenly stopped. She put a hand to her mouth.

Sam heard her mother take a sharp breath. She looked ahead and saw what they saw. There, in the clearing, was a small wooden stable. It reminded Sam of the kind of stable she'd seen in Christmas scenes: three walls and an open front with an A-shaped roof over the top. In the middle of the stable stood a short post with a shelf. Sitting on the shelf sat a painted wooden statue of

Mary holding the Baby Jesus.

Lizzy, Sam, and their mom slowly approached the statue. It was hand-carved and crudely painted. Mary wore a blue robe and white veil over her head. The Baby Jesus looked golden, with a brown tunic covering his body. Chubby arms reached up and chubby legs stretched down, with one foot over the top of the other.

It's the way Jesus looks on a cross, Sam thought as she imagined the crucifix back at St. Clare's.

"We should pray," Lizzy said.

The three of them knelt down and bowed their heads to pray silently.

The only prayer that Sam thought seemed right was "Hail, Mary, full of grace . . ."

Sam looked up and noticed handwriting carved into the wall behind the post. The words were foreign. She thought they might be Latin. *"Exitus"* stood out. Underneath the words, she saw a mix of letters with *M* and *C* and *D* and *L* and some *X*'s and *I*'s. She wondered if they were someone's initials.

Her mother stood up and took out her phone. Sam heard the "click" of the phone's camera. Then she knelt again.

Sam found it hard to take her eyes off the statue of Mary and the Baby Jesus. She had the feeling that she had been given a special honor being there.

The light began to fade, as if the sun was setting. Sam wasn't sure of the

time, but she couldn't believe they'd been there all day. Or had they?

"It's time to go," Sam's mom said.

The three stood up and followed the path back to the trail. Sam kept looking back, but it was as if the shrine had faded into the woods.

When they reached the trail, the sky and woods looked as bright as they should have in the middle of the day. Sam glanced down and noticed that the path seemed to be covered up with pine needles and leaves. It was as if it never existed.

No one said anything. Sam felt like words would somehow ruin the moment.

They walked for several minutes down the trail. Sam heard noises ahead and saw a small group of people coming their way. There was a man with shaggy hair and a beard. He carried a baby in a carrier on his back. A woman walked next to him, along with a little boy and a little girl behind her.

As they passed each other, Sam's mom said hello and the family said hello back. They walked on.

Then, suddenly, the man called out from behind them. "Excuse me," he said.

Mrs. Perry and the girls turned.

The man came up to her and said, "I'm sorry to bother you, but . . . you help out at the soup kitchen, don't you?"

"That's right," Sam's mom said.

"Maybe you don't remember me, but I—*we*—came in a month or so ago," the man said. He reached for her hand and shook it.

Mrs. Perry smiled. "I thought you looked familiar."

The woman stepped up next to the man. "You're Belle," she said.

"I'd lost my job," the man said. "I

couldn't feed my family. We were thrown out of our apartment. The soup kitchen was all we had. And I remember how you made it so I didn't feel ashamed to be there."

The little boy and girl came up and hid behind the man's legs, peeking out at Sam and Lizzy with shy looks.

The woman's eyes were tear-filled. "Your job placement service helped my husband find a job."

"Did it work out for you?" Mrs. Perry asked.

"Oh, yes," he said. "I've been working steady. And today is the first time in a long time we've been able to do anything as a family. So we're taking a hike."

"Beautiful day for it," Mrs. Perry said. Sam thought she was blushing.

The woman suddenly stepped forward and hugged Sam's mother. "Thank you," she said.

The family turned and continued on their hike.

Mrs. Perry didn't move. She watched them walk away. Then she put a hand on Sam's shoulder. "Sometimes all we can see is the work. This is the joy."

***

That evening, the Perry family gathered around to look at the pictures of the shrine on Mrs. Perry's phone.

The photos Mrs. Perry had taken on her phone showed a clearing encircled by trees. But there was no shrine.

—.—

CHAPTER THIRTEEN

Be Ye Glad

The next week at school felt like the end of the year. Displays on the bulletin boards were slowly taken down. Pictures of the presidents of the United States that had looked fuzzy to Nick were now sharp and clear. President Martin Van Buren no longer looked like a koala. Nick was happy that he hadn't been teased very much about his glasses. Clara, a girl in the other third-grade glass, even said he looked "cute." That caused more teasing than the glasses.

Nick sat at his desk and noticed the empty walls. No more posters about the lives of the saints. They had been rolled up and put away. The art projects were sent home. Riley had offered for Sister Lucy to keep his giant picture of Big Foot. She gently said it would be better hanging in his bedroom. She didn't want anything to happen to it during the summer.

"It's like a toy winding down," Nick had said to Brad. Final projects were handed in. Quizzes and tests were taken. Life seemed to drain from each classroom. It was as if they were just big cold rooms when the kids weren't there.

Meanwhile, the church grounds were set up for the Be Ye Glad Spring Festival. Wooden booths were lined up, along with small tents and tables, for homemade crafts and face-painting and baked goods and candy. Some of the tents were set up for contests and games.

The field on the other side of the church was freshly laid out for the softball tournament.

Every day at recess the kids watched the progress. Nick had to admit that he was feeling more and more excited about the big day.

On the Saturday morning of the festival, the Perry kids went with their father to help set up tables and chairs. Lizzy and Sam tried to dress in costumes that made them look like ladies from the time of Robin Hood. Andrew found a green hat and stuck a feather in it. Nick refused to put on a costume. He said he'd feel silly looking like a Robin Hood with glasses. Instead he wore a belt with a small plastic sword on the side. It was from a *Lord of the Rings* costume he'd worn for Halloween a couple of years before.

Brad eventually showed up with his

parents. He and Nick watched as an inflatable castle of blue and yellow was hooked up to loud machines and pumped full of air.

A dunking booth was built, and the tank filled with water.

Maureen Sullivan, Mr. Norm's sister, arrived with a long trailer. She put up a makeshift fence for a petting zoo. Then she brought out a pony, a couple of sheep, goats, a small pig, and a llama. Nick looked for Chaser, the spirited donkey he met during last year's Christmas pageant, but Mrs. Sullivan said she was afraid he might get away and ruin the festival.

People slowly arrived throughout the morning. Riley showed up looking as much like Robin Hood as anybody could. He had on a green felt hat and a matching tunic and brown leggings and even shoes that looked like slippers. He had a bow slung on one shoulder and a

strap holding a satchel over the other.

"It's called a 'quiver,'" he told Nick. Sticks stuck out of the top of the quiver.

"Are those real arrows?" Nick asked.

"My dad wouldn't let me bring real arrows," Riley said. He was clearly disappointed. "They're just sticks that I glued some little brushes on."

A small platform had been set up with speakers to play music. Father Cliff stepped up and was handed a microphone. There was a high-pitched squeal of feedback. The crowd went silent.

Father Cliff laughed. "I guess that got your attention." He thanked everyone for coming and made some announcements about all of the booths and activities. Nick didn't know until then that the festival was supposed to raise money to help the school. Father Cliff led them in prayer for the day and then said, "Everybody have fun!"

And so they did.

***

Early in the afternoon, a group of girls had taken over the inflatable castle. Riley wanted to go in and jump, but Natalie, a tall girl from the other third-grade class, kept stopping him.

Nick and Brad watched Riley and thought it was funny. Riley came over to them in a fury.

"All the boys should storm the castle," Riley said. "Boys against girls."

Brad thought it was a good idea.

Nick wasn't so sure. "It's only the three of us against ten girls."

"We need more boys," Riley said and then announced, "They'll be my 'Men of the Greenwood'!" He ran off to find them.

It didn't take long. Most of the boys from the two third-grade classes agreed to join in. They gathered in a large group around Riley. He gave them battle orders. "We'll circle around the castle and when I shout, we run in.

"But there's only that front door," one of the boys said. "Natalie will kill us. She's strong. *I know*." The boy looked as if he was truly scared of her.

"There are flaps and nets on the other sides," Riley told them. "They're held down by Velcro. Just pull them up and you can get in."

Nick had a nagging feeling that this was a bad idea. But it was better than standing around waiting for the girls to get bored of jumping in the castle.

The boys did as Riley had said. They circled around the yellow-and-blue castle.

Nick could see Sam bouncing inside. He imagined the look of surprise on her face when they attacked.

Riley moved around to the side that had a slide into the castle. Nick watched as he put a hand on the lowest rung of the inflated ladder. He looked around with a wild look on his face. Then he shouted, "Now!"

The boys rushed at the castle with a roar. The girls inside saw them coming and shrieked. Natalie stood in front of the little entrance with her arms folded. There was a lot of pushing and shoving between her and two boys.

Nick and Brad went around to the side and found one of the flaps Riley had talked about. They pulled with all their might and the flap lifted up. They started to crawl in. A couple of girls nearby lost their balance and fell

onto Brad. Nick scrambled in another direction and stumbled into Sam's legs. She toppled onto him.

"What are you doing?" she shouted.

"Storming the castle," he gasped. He rolled off to the side and got stuck between the bouncy bottom and the side wall.

Sam crawled over to him. "This is crazy!" she said.

There was a lot of screaming and confusion and laughing and bouncing.

Then Riley appeared at the top of the slide. "Aha!" he shouted and put his hands on his hips. *He's trying to look like Robin Hood*, Nick thought. But the shelf at the top of the slide was made of the same stuff as the rest of the castle and his legs wobbled. He tipped to one side and then the other.

Then Nick saw that Riley was still wearing his quiver with the arrows sticking out of the top. *Uh oh*, Nick thought and shouted, "No! Stop!"

Riley smiled at him and waved. Then he lost his footing and fell sideways down the slide. He tumbled onto the bottom.

Some of the girls shouted, "Get him!"

Suddenly a swarm of girls threw themselves onto Riley. He screamed and then laughed. The girls were tickling him.

Then, just as suddenly, he started shouting, "Get off! Get off!" He pushed them away.

He sounded so serious that both the girls and boys spread out. He struggled onto his knees and looked down. There were gashes and slices in the bed of the castle. Riley's arrows had torn through the surface when the girls jumped on him.

Nick gulped hard. He thought he could hear air hissing out of the gashes.

"Everybody get out!" someone yelled.

The kids screamed. It looked like nothing but knees and elbows as they crawled and bounced for ways out.

Nick could hear adult voices shouting now.

By the time he and Sam had crawled out, the castle was losing air. It tilted a little to the side.

Brad came alongside Nick and said, "Well, *that* was a surprise."

The grown-ups were not happy. The boys were in trouble. Riley got an earful for going into the castle with sticks, even though they weren't very pointy. He was told that he should have known better. Riley agreed. He should have. He wasn't thinking.

Father Cliff stood next to the deflating castle. He shook his head with his hand on his chin. Nick heard him say, "The rental company won't be happy."

***

Sam wandered the festival grounds with Kim. She saw her mother near one of the booths with baked goods. They smiled and waved to each other.

"She looks happy," Kim said.

"I think our hike helped," Sam said. "Mom said it helped give her 'perspective.'" Sam said the word "perspective" slowly.

"What is 'perspective'?" Kim asked.

"I think it's looking at things in the right way," Sam said. She was trying to repeat what she'd heard her mother say.

"So it's like *joy*," Kim said.

Sam thought about that. "Maybe it's easier to have joy when we look at things the right way."

The girls passed a booth that had bowling balls and rings set up inside. A table in front had softballs. Stuffed animals hung from the ceiling.

"Three throws for twenty-five cents,"

the woman inside said. "All the money helps the school. And you could win a toy."

"Go on," Kim said. She had reached into her pocket and put a quarter on the table.

"You go," said Sam.

Kim insisted, "You throw better than I do."

Sam picked up a ball. She aimed and threw it at a bowling pin. The ball knocked it over. Then she threw a ball at a ring. It went through without touching the sides. She threw the third ball at a stick with a plastic bottle on top. She knocked the bottle off.

"You're good," the woman in the booth said.

Then a hand slapped against the table. "Here's a dollar for her to throw again," a voice said.

Sam looked up. Mr. Hildreth smiled at her.

Sam backed up. "No, thanks," she said.

"Go on," Mr. Hildreth said. "I'll bet you can hit everything you aim at."

"Do it," Kim whispered.

"The money helps the school," Mr. Hildreth added.

"But you'll make me play softball," Sam said to him.

Mr. Hildreth shook his head. "No pressure," he told her. "I just want to see your talent before you lose it."

"Lose it?" Sam asked.

"By not using it," he said. He gave her a sharp look. "You have twelve throws."

Sam couldn't decide what to do.

"You can do it," the woman said.

"Okay," Sam said.

She threw the twelve balls and missed only twice. One miss was because Kim tickled her. The second miss was because she realized a crowd had gathered around to watch and it made her nervous.

Mr. Hildreth made *tsking* sounds with his tongue. "It's a waste if you don't play ball," he said and walked away.

Sam wondered if he was right.

CHAPTER FOURTEEN

The Big Game

The third graders were scheduled to play in the softball tournament at four o'clock. Most of the kids had gathered earlier to watch the other grades play. Nick stepped up just as Mr. Hildreth was picking the two teams. He felt someone brush against his arm. It was Sam.

"Are you playing?" she asked.

"No," he replied. "Are you?"

"No," she said.

Mr. Hildreth suddenly barked, "We have a problem. Riley's dad took him home. I guess because he ruined the castle."

Some of the kids laughed.

"I need another player," he said. He shot a look at Sam. "That should be you, Samantha Perry."

Sam took a few steps back and shook her head. "I don't want to play."

Nick said, "You should."

She gave him a hard look. "I don't *want* to."

"Okay, Nick. You're in," Mr. Hildreth said. "Maybe your new glasses will help."

Nick shook his head.

Brad broke from the crowd and grabbed Nick's arm. "Don't be a baby. It's for fun anyway." He dragged Nick to their team.

"I didn't bring a glove," Nick protested.

"You can borrow one," Brad said.

Sister Lucy stood nearby. She nodded to him. "You can do it," she said.

Nick looked back at Sam. She waved her hand at him to go on.

What happened next was a blur to

Nick. Mr. Hildreth put him in right field. Nick was thankful he had the glasses to see everything. He was also thankful that no one could hit that far.

Then, in the third inning, a boy named Russell hit the ball hard. It popped up high to Nick. Nick rushed to get under it.

"Please, please, please let me catch it," he whispered as the ball began to drop. If he caught it, he wouldn't have to throw it. If he missed . . .

Nick groaned. The ball had gone further than he thought. He had moved forward and now he had to back up *fast*. He raised his arm. The ball hit the side of his glove and fell to the ground.

"Second base! Second base!" the kids were screaming.

Nick darted around to get the ball. He picked it up and threw it as hard as he could. He hoped he had thrown it in the right direction.

He hadn't.

The ball went to first base while Russell reached second base.

Nick heard laughter and loud groans.

"It's okay," he heard Mr. Hildreth shout. "It's what I expected."

Nick wanted to throw his glove down and quit. "I *knew* it," he said to himself.

He saw his dad standing on the sidelines. "You're good!" his dad called out. "Play for fun. Don't take it seriously."

Later in the game, Nick's team was at their turn to bat. Nick was far down in the lineup because he was the last to join. *At the rate they're going, I won't bat at all,* he thought. He decided that was a good thing. He didn't want to look any more stupid than he already did.

His family gathered around. They were talking to him, but he wasn't really listening. *They're saying the kinds of encouraging things families always say*, he thought.

"You're up!" Mr. Hildreth shouted.

It took a moment for Nick to realize the coach was talking to him.

"Me?" Nick asked. His mouth went dry. His heart began to pound.

"Come on!" Mr. Hildreth said. "Get it over with."

Nick picked up a bat and went to the plate. The boy named Russell was the pitcher for the other team. He smiled at Nick. Nick lifted the bat and took his stance.

"Strike one!" Mr. Hildreth called out from behind him. Nick had swung at the ball and missed.

Then it was "Ball one!" and then "Foul ball!" and then another strike.

"Can you *see* the ball?" Mr. Hildreth yelled.

Suddenly his father was running toward him from the sidelines.

"What now?" Mr. Hildreth said.

Mr. Perry put a hand on Nick's shoulder and leaned in. "You're not trying," he said softly. "Remember: You may have a hard time with throwing. But that doesn't mean you can't hit the ball."

His dad ran off again. Nick realized that his father was right. Nick *hadn't* been trying to hit the ball. He was swinging the bat just to put an end to his suffering. He wasn't very good at baseball, he'd decided. There was no point in making the effort.

"Play ball!" Mr. Hildreth yelled.

Nick knew he had nothing to lose.

Russell pitched the ball to him. Nick didn't swing at it.

"Ball two!" Mr. Hildreth called out and threw the ball back. "Over the *plate*, Russell!"

Russell pitched again.

Nick saw the ball coming at him in slow motion, just like the moment when he broke the window. He swung the bat around and hit the softball solidly. He didn't move as it sailed high over Russell's head and into the left field.

"Run!" Mr. Hildreth yelled at him.

Nick took off for first base.

The ball had flown past Natalie in left field.

Nick tagged first base and was running for second when Mr. Hildreth shouted, "The ball's out of the field! Home run! It's a home run!"

Nick glanced to his right. Natalie was running, but the ball was somewhere out of sight.

Nick saw his family jumping up and down on the sidelines. Sister Lucy and Brad and the rest of his team were screaming. He felt his cheeks burning

as he rounded third base and headed for home.

He didn't feel like a loser after all.

***

For Nick, the rest of the festival felt like a big celebration. There were pats on the back and hugs and compliments and Brad even said he was a "legend" for being the only third-grader to hit a home run that day.

Though, later on, Nick thought something even better had happened.

Some of the teachers took turns sitting in the dunking booth. Nick, Sam, and Kim happened to walk past just as Mr. Hildreth climbed in and sat down on the seat above the tank.

Nick looked at Sam.

Sam shook her head. "It costs a dollar. I don't have one."

"I do," said Kim. She ran over to Deacon Chuck. He was taking the money for the dunking booth.

Deacon Chuck gave Kim three softballs to throw.

"She's throwing?" Mr. Hildreth called out from his chair. "I won't even get my feet wet."

Then Kim handed the balls to Sam.

Sam took her place in front of the round target.

"Hey! Wait a minute! I want out!" Mr. Hildreth said and pretended like he was going to get off of the chair.

"The money goes to the school!" Sam shouted at him.

Mr. Hildreth grinned at her. "Now I'm in trouble," he said.

Sam had three chances to dunk the gym teacher. She hit the target on the first throw. A loud bell rang, and the seat dropped. Into the water went Mr. Hildreth with a huge splash.

A crowd cheered.

Mr. Hildreth came up, sputtering

and spraying water. He pulled himself up and leaned on the edge of the tank. "I deserved that," he said to Sam.

Sam smiled at him. "I know," she said.

Nick laughed and thought, *What a good day.*

CHAPTER FIFTEEN

—·—

Again I Say Rejoice

On the last day of the school year, Sister Lucy handed out certificates to each of the students.

"These are awards for your participation in class," Sister Lucy said.

Some of the kids were awarded for asking the best questions or giving the best answers. Some were awarded for their manners. Brad was awarded for riding Chaser the Donkey. Sam was awarded for winning the spelling bee. Riley was awarded for trying to find Big Foot. Nick was awarded for "Best Adventures," and the list included riding Chaser the Donkey with Brad, encountering a mountain lion, and saving Riley from the ice.

"That's quite a year," Sister Lucy said.

Sam looked over at her brother. He was grinning from ear to ear.

Father Cliff came in to say a few words. He reminded them of their First Communion and how important that was to their lives. Then he announced that the school had a new third-grade teacher joining them. "Sister Lucy is moving on," he said.

The kids groaned.

Sam said "No!" louder than she meant to. How could Sister Lucy leave St. Clare's?

Sister Lucy held up her hands for them to be quiet.

Father Cliff was smiling. "I didn't say she was leaving. She just won't be teaching third grade," he said. He turned to her.

Sister Lucy stepped forward. "I'll be teaching *fourth* grade," she said.

It took a moment for the kids to realize what she'd said. Sam's jaw dropped.

"I'll be teaching some of you next year," Sister Lucy added.

Cheers and shouts erupted.

Sam looked around at all the happy faces. Then something caught the corner of her eye and she looked to the back of the class. The door there had opened. Kim's uncle and aunt crept into the room. Kim's uncle saw Sam and put a finger to his lips.

Sam turned around. Kim was still looking forward at Sister Lucy with a big smile.

Sam looked back at Kim's uncle and aunt. Her uncle now had a phone in his hand. He lifted it up.

"And now we have a special presentation," Father Cliff said from the front of the room.

Sam spun around.

Father Cliff said, "Some guests have come from far away to be here." He gestured to Kim. "Kim Lee. Please stand up."

"What?" Kim said. Her eyes were wide with shock. "What is this?" she asked as she stood up.

Sister Lucy moved next to Kim and put an arm around her. Kim looked at her, confused.

Father Cliff continued, "God does great things, often when we don't expect it."

He looked at the door. A Chinese man and woman slowly walked into the class. Both had gray hair and glasses. The man wore a dark suit and the woman had on a pale yellow dress. They smiled at Kim.

Kim let out a loud gasp and looked like her legs might give out. Both hands went to her mouth. Sam heard her

screech and then utter something like a whimper.

The woman shuffled to Kim and held out her arms.

"*Mama! Baba!*" Kim cried out in a voice choked by tears. She sprung forward into the woman's arms. The man wrapped his arms around them both. Soft words were spoken in Chinese among the sniffles and tears.

"This is Li Wei and Wang Xiu Ying, Kim's father and mother from China," Father Cliff explained to the class. "They have been imprisoned for their faith for a long time. The Chinese government freed them a week ago and have let them come to America."

Kim's uncle and aunt came to the front and joined the family embraces. Kim's uncle still held his phone to film the event.

Sam began to cry. So did some of the other kids in the class.

Kim clung to her parents as if she would never let them go.

Rejoice always, Sam thought. *Again, I say rejoice.*

***

Nick and Sam stood together in front of the Old Perry House. A large moving truck sat in the driveway. Movers in gray overalls went back and forth from the truck to the house carrying boxes and furniture. They reminded Nick of busy ants.

Nick's parents darted in and out of the front door, giving directions to what went where.

The four Perry kids were warned to stay clear until the movers were done.

Andrew and Lizzy sat under the tall maple tree near the side of the house. Lizzy was drawing in her notepad. Andrew was watching the movers when he wasn't reading the book in his lap.

"Maybe I'll go over to Kim's," Sam said.

"Have you met her parents?" Nick asked.

Sam nodded. "Kim's mom is sick. That's why the government set them free."

"Sick with what?" Nick asked.

"I don't know. But I think she'll get help from doctors here that they don't have in China." She looked at the movers. "I can't wait to get into my room."

"It'll be a while," Nick said.

Sam kicked at a small stone and strolled over to their mom.

Nick thought his mom looked happy. He'd heard that a lot of people who went to the festival signed up to help at the soup kitchen.

The warmth of the sun felt like hands on his shoulders and he almost expected an excited voice to whisper, "Summer is here!"

He smiled at the thought of the days to come.